THE MAGICAL MERMAID

and

Kate Crackernuts

Retold by MARGARET MAYO

Illustrated by PETER BAILEY

For Natalie
M.M.
With love to the two young whippersnappers,
Oscar and Felix
P.B.

Orchard Books
96 Leonard Street, London EC2A 4XD
Orchard Books Australia
32/45-51 Huntley Street, Alexandria, NSW 2015
The text was first published in Great Britain in the form
of a gift collection called *The Orchard Book of Magical Tales*
and *The Orchard Book of Mythical Birds and Beasts*
illustrated by Jane Ray, in 1993 and 1996
This edition first published in hardback in 2003
First paperback publication in 2004

A CIP catalogue record for this book is available from the British Library
ISBN 1 84362 083 9 (hardback)
ISBN 1 84362 091 x (paperback)
1 3 5 7 9 10 8 6 4 2 (hardback)
1 3 5 7 9 10 8 6 4 2 (paperback)
Printed in Great Britain

CONTENTS

THE MAGICAL MERMAID

Once there was a young fisherman called Lutey, and one day he met a mermaid, face to face. Now that's a rare thing to happen to anyone. And it's rarer still to meet a mermaid and live to tell the tale. But he did.

Lutey lived in a cottage overlooking the sea, together with his wife, three lively sons and a large, brown, lolloping and most affectionate dog called Towser. And it just so happened that one morning Lutey went for a stroll down on the beach, with Towser at his heels.

The tide was out, and the rippled sands were still wet. The only sound was the lap-lapping of the waves as they rolled ashore. Then, all of a sudden, Lutey heard a strange, mournful cry: "*Aaa-ooooo!*" It was coming from behind some rocks that jutted out into the beach. What could it be?

Lutey hurried forward. Behind the rocks was a shallow pool, fringed by more rocks and separated from the sea by a

wide stretch of sand. Lutey gasped. He couldn't believe his eyes. There, sitting on the rocks, was a *mermaid*. She was the most beautiful creature he had ever seen. Her skin was white and smooth as marble. She had long golden hair and a wonderful, curving, greenish-blue tail that shimmered softly in the morning sun.

As soon as she saw him, she called out, "Have pity, good man, and help me."

Lutey knew that mermaids were unlucky creatures. He knew the fisherman's saying: "Don't ever look at a mermaid!" But she was so beautiful he couldn't take his eyes off her.

"My name is Lutey," he said, "but who are you? And how can I help you?"

"I am Morvena," she answered. "And I've been sitting here so busy combing my hair and gazing at myself in the water that I didn't notice the tide go out. Now I can't get back to the sea unless...unless, Lutey, you carry me across the sands. If you do, I'll pay you well."

Lutey laughed. "What can you possibly give to me?"

"I can give you three wishes," she answered.

"Three wishes! Oh! I know what I want! I've often thought about it!" exclaimed Lutey. "Not money. No. Nothing like that."

"Think carefully," said the mermaid. "*Very carefully*. Then choose what you want."

"What I would like," said Lutey quietly, "is the power to heal people when they're sick and make them well and strong again."

"A healer. The gift is yours," she said. "And what else?"

"I would like," he said, "the power to break wicked spells that make folk angry so they end up quarrelling and hurting one another."

"A peacemaker. The gift is yours," she said. "And one more?"

"I would like these powers to continue after I die," said Lutey. "I would like them to pass down through my family, for always."

"The gift is yours," she said. "So now carry me to the sea." She reached out her white arms and wrapped them round Lutey's neck. But as he lifted her, Towser began to whine. It was a long, low and eerie whine.

Then Lutey was afraid. "How can I know you won't harm me?" he asked.

Morvena touched her hair and took out a golden comb, all delicately patterned and set with tiny pearls. "Take this as a token," she said. And she smiled at him, and Lutey forgot his fear.

"That's a real beauty!" he said as he slipped it into his trouser pocket where he kept various bits and pieces – some string, a pocket-knife and such like.

And then Morvena began to sing. She sang about secret caves and enchanted palaces under the sea. She sang about a life free from pain, death and sadness. As though in a dream, Lutey began to walk across the sands, and his dog Towser followed, still whining. But Lutey had ears only for the mermaid and her songs.

He reached the sea and waded in. But Towser didn't follow. He stayed at the water's edge, still whining. Lutey waded on, until the water reached the top of his legs.

"Now you can swim off," he said.

"Deeper, deeper," sang Morvena. "Take me deeper."

He waded on until the water reached his waist. "Now swim off," he said.

But Morvena only sang, "Deeper, deeper ...take me deeper."

He waded on until the water reached his shoulders. "I can go no further," he said, and tried to lower her into the water. But she wrapped her arms more tightly round his neck and wound her tail about his legs and sang in his ear.

"Come, come...come with me," she sang. And she sang and sang and sang, until the only thing Lutey wanted was to go with her.

And then Towser barked. Again and again he barked, loud and fierce, until the shore echoed with his barking. At last Lutey heard him and looked back and saw his large, brown, lolloping and most affectionate dog by the water's edge. Lutey looked beyond, and saw his three lively sons and his own dear wife standing by the cottage door.

"Let me go!" he cried. "I cannot leave my family and come with you!"

But Morvena only tightened her grasp and tried to pull his head down into the water. Lutey struggled, but though the mermaid was light and seemed quite fragile, her power was greater than his.

But there was still something he could do. He felt in his trouser pocket and pulled out his knife. He flicked it open and held it above the water. “By the power of iron,” he cried, “let me go.”

Immediately she loosened her hold. "Ah, Lutey," she sighed, "you were cleverer than I thought. You knew that the power of iron is greater than all enchantments." Slowly she swam around him. "Farewell, my lovely man," she said. "Farewell for nine long years...and then we shall meet again." And with that she sank below the waves.

Lutey was trembling. It seemed as if his strength had been sucked out of him. But he took a deep breath, slipped his pocket-knife back in its usual place and waded back towards the land.

When he reached the shore, there was Towser lolloping around him, leaping up and licking him all over and doing a lot of tail-wagging. Lutey patted him fondly. "Good dog!" he said. "Without you I would have been lost!"

Of course, when Lutey reached his own cottage, wet through to the skin, there was some explaining to be done.

"What happened?" asked his wife.

"It's a long story," answered Lutey. "Wait until I'm warm and dry, and then I'll tell it."

A little later, sitting by the fire warming himself, Lutey told his wife and his wide-eyed sons about the mermaid, and at the end he took the comb out of his pocket.

"So the story is true," whispered his wife. "But the three wishes, I wonder, will they come true?"

They did. Lutey discovered that whenever anyone was sick, somehow he knew which herbs and juices and powders to mix together to make the right medicine to cure that person. Even his touch had healing power.

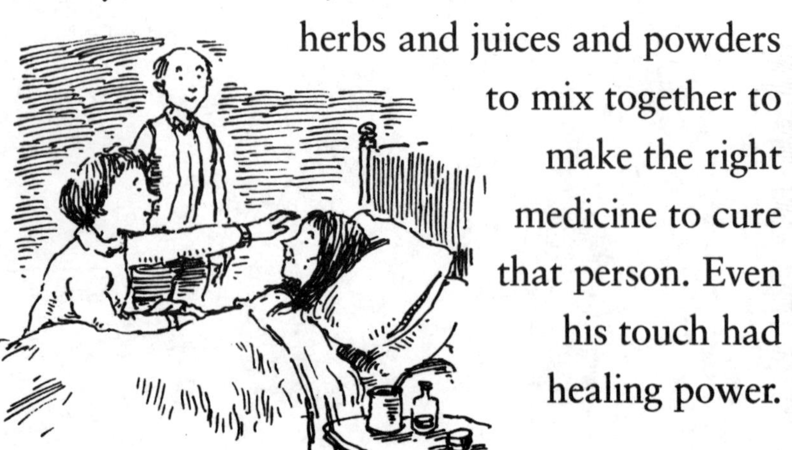

Besides this, Lutey became a peacemaker. Whenever there were quarrels, stealing and fights, people came to Lutey, and somehow he knew the truth and made peace.

News of his gifts spread far and wide, and men, women and children travelled many, many miles to seek his help. And Lutey gave it freely. So he never grew rich. He just stayed a fisherman who loved the sea and fishing, and as his sons grew older, they became fishermen too.

Nine years passed. Nine happy years. But then, late one evening, Lutey went out fishing with Tom, his eldest son, in their small boat.

There was no wind. The sea was calm and still...until, without any warning, a gigantic wave came rolling towards them. Lutey and Tom held on tight while it tossed their small boat up and down. Then as soon as the wave had passed,

a mermaid rose up from the water. It was Morvena.

"The time has come," she sang. "Now you are mine, Lutey, my lovely man."

Slowly, silently, Lutey rose to his feet, plunged into the water and was gone. And slowly, silently, the mermaid sank below the waves. The last Tom saw of them was Morvena's long golden hair spread across the water, and then that too was gone.

Lutey was never seen again. But, from that time on, Tom, his eldest son, had the gift of healing, and he too became a peacemaker. And these gifts passed on down, through Lutey's family, even to this day.

But Morvena claims a high price for the gifts. Every nine years, regular as sea tides, one of Lutey's descendants is lost at sea and never seen again. Perhaps they have gone to join Lutey and the mermaid in the enchanted world under the sea. No one knows for sure.

An English tale

KATE CRACKERNUTS

Long, long ago, there lived a bonnie princess and her name was Kate. Now it happened that her mother died, and when her father married again, the new queen already had a daughter of her own, and her name also was Kate. So there they were – two Kates in the same family. And it would have been confusing, if it wasn't that the king's Kate was by far the bonnier of the two. So nearly everyone called her Bonnie Kate, while the queen's daughter they called Kate. Just Kate.

Right from the start, the two Kates were friends and loved one another like true sisters. But the queen was bitterly jealous of Bonnie Kate's handsome looks and full of anger that the king's daughter was bonnier than her own. One day she could bear it no longer and went to see the hen-wife, an old witch who kept a flock of hens not far from the castle gates. And the queen asked her to cast a spell on the king's daughter that would spoil her beauty.

"Send the lassie to me," said the hen-wife, "without a bite to eat or a drop to drink, and I'll soon hash up her bonnie face."

So, early next morning, the queen sent the king's daughter to the hen-wife to fetch a basket of eggs for breakfast. But on her way through the kitchen, Bonnie

Kate saw some oatcakes on the table, and she picked one up and off she went munching it. When she came to the hen-wife's house and asked for the eggs, the hen-wife said, "Now lift the lid of that pot there and see what you can see."

Bonnie Kate lifted the lid of the black pot that hung over the fire, and a cloud of steam rose up. A cloud of steam and nothing more. And the hen-wife said, "Go home to the queen and tell her to keep her larder door better locked!

Well, next morning the queen once again sent Bonnie Kate to fetch a basket of eggs. Bonnie Kate went through the kitchen, and the table was bare. She tried the larder, and the door was locked. But as she walked along the road, she saw an old man picking peas, and being a friendly lass she stopped for a chat. Then the old man gave her a handful of pods, and off she went munching peas.

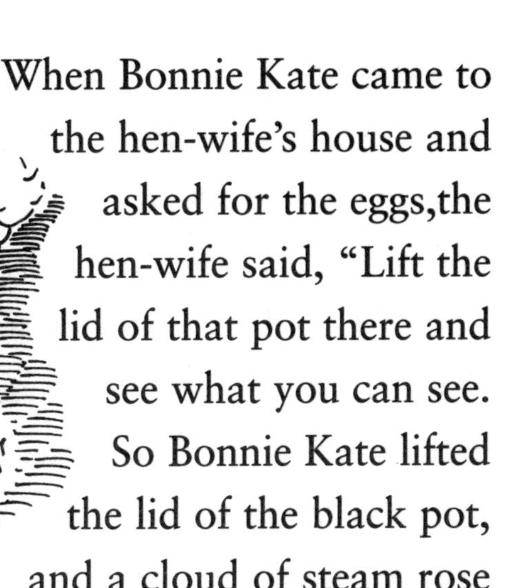

When Bonnie Kate came to the hen-wife's house and asked for the eggs,the hen-wife said, "Lift the lid of that pot there and see what you can see.

So Bonnie Kate lifted the lid of the black pot, and a cloud of steam rose up. A cloud of steam and nothing more.

And the hen-wife said, "Go home to the queen and tell her that if she wants something done, she must come herself!"

Well, next morning the queen herself woke Bonnie Kate and didn't let her out of sight; and she kept beside her every step of the way to the hen-wife's house.

When they got there, once again the hen-wife said, "Now lift the lid off that pot there and see what you can see."

Bonnie Kate lifted the lid, and then...a sheep's head rose up out of the pot and jumped on to her shoulders and covered her own bonnie head entirely. So there she was with a sheep's head instead of her own.

Then the queen was satisfied.

But the other Kate, the queen's own daughter, was angry – very angry – when she saw what had happened to her sister, and said to her, "We can no longer stay here! Who knows what may happen to you next!" And she picked up a fine linen cloth, wrapped it round her sister's head, and took her by the hand. Then together they set out to seek their fortune.

They walked far, they walked further than far, until they came at last to another kingdom. Then Kate went boldly to the king's castle and found work as a kitchen maid; and, in return, she and her sick sister were given food and allowed to sleep in a small room in the attic.

Now the king had two sons, and the elder of the two was ill and no one knew what ailed him. Day in, day out, he lay in his bed and he slept. And the strange thing was that anyone who sat and watched over him at night disappeared and was never seen again. So the time came when there was no one left brave enough to sit with the prince at night.

When Kate heard about this, she said, "I'll do that. For a bag full of silver, I'll sit with the prince."

And the king agreed.

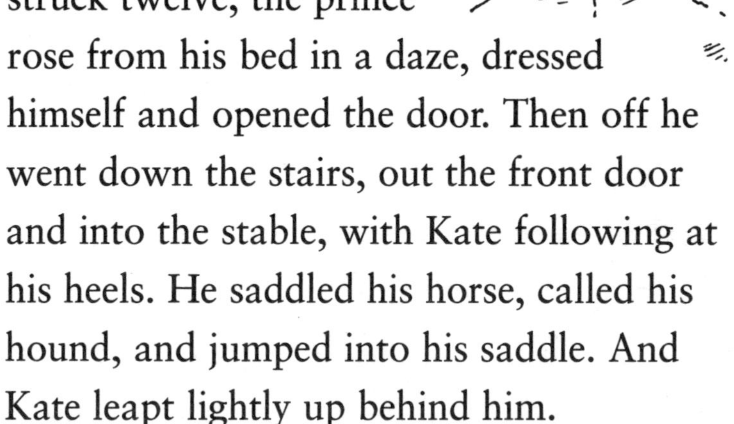

So that night Kate sat with the sleeping prince. All went well until midnight. But when the castle clock struck twelve, the prince rose from his bed in a daze, dressed himself and opened the door. Then off he went down the stairs, out the front door and into the stable, with Kate following at his heels. He saddled his horse, called his hound, and jumped into his saddle. And Kate leapt lightly up behind him.

Away they rode with the hound running alongside. They came to a wood of close-growing hazel, and as they wound in and out amongst the trees, Kate picked hazelnuts from the branches and filled her apron pockets with them.

They rode on until they came to a green hill, and then the prince called out, "Open, open, green hill, and let the young prince in with his horse and hound."

"And," added Kate, "his fair lady behind him."

A door opened in the hillside, and they entered a magnificent hall that was brightly lit and full of handsome people dancing to the liveliest, most toe-tapping music Kate had ever heard.

Now as soon as they were inside, Kate slipped off the horse and hid in the shadows near the door. Immediately some beautiful ladies surrounded the prince and led him off to the dance. The prince danced with each beautiful lady in turn. He danced and he danced. He did not rest for a moment.

Then Kate knew that she was in the hall of the fairy folk, and she knew too that she must be careful, for if they caught her spying on them they would never ever let her go. So she drew back and hid herself in the darkest shadows she could find.

After a while she happened to notice a fairy child playing with a silver wand, and then she heard one of the fairy women say, "You take care of that wand. Three

strokes from it, just three, would make that poor wee lassie with the sheep's head as bonnie as ever she was!"

So Kate took some hazelnuts out of her pocket and rolled them towards the fairy child. She rolled them and she rolled them until the child dropped the wand and chased after the nuts. Quickly Kate crept forward, snatched up the wand and hid it under her apron.

Then the cock crowed. The prince came and mounted his horse, and Kate leapt lightly up behind him, and they rode back to the castle with the hound running alongside.

When the horse was in the stable, and the prince once more asleep in his bed, Kate sat down by the fire and cracked some nuts and ate them.

In the morning the king, the queen and the prince's younger brother came to the room, and Kate told them that the prince had had a good night. That was all.

The king asked Kate to watch over his son for yet another night.

"I'll do that," Kate said. "For a bag of gold, I'll sit with the prince."

Now the moment they had all gone, Kate took her wand and hurried up to the attic room to find her sister. She touched her three times with the wand and, there and then, the sheep's head disappeared and her sister was as bonnie as ever she was!

The next night came, and the same things happened as before. When the castle clock struck twelve, the prince rose from his bed, dressed, went down the stairs and out the front door, saddled his horse and called his hound. He mounted and Kate leapt up behind him. They took the winding path through the woods and Kate picked hazelnuts and filled her apron pockets. They came to the green hill, and the prince said, "Open, open, green hill and let the young prince in with his horse and hound."

"And," added Kate, "his fair lady behind him."

The door swung open, and they entered the hall where the beautiful dancers danced and the fiddlers played. Again Kate hid in the shadows, while the prince danced without resting for a moment.

After a while, Kate noticed a fairy child playing with a white bird, chasing it and catching it. Then she heard one of the fairy women say, "You take care of that bird. Three bites of it, just three, would set the prince free from our fairy enchantment and make him as well as ever he was."

So Kate took some hazelnuts out of her pocket and rolled them towards the child. She rolled them and she rolled them until the child let go of the bird and chased after them. Quickly Kate crept forward, snatched up the bird and hid it under her apron.

Then the cock crowed, and the prince mounted his horse, and Kate leapt up behind him. And they were off, back to the palace, with the hound running alongside.

When the horse was in the stable, and the prince once more asleep in his bed, Kate killed the bird, plucked off its feathers, and hung it over the fire to roast. Before long a rich, savoury smell filled the room. And then the prince woke up.

"Oh!" he said. "I'd like a taste of that bird!" So Kate gave him a bite.

He rose up on his elbow and, by and by, he said, "Oh! I'd like another taste of that bird!"

So Kate gave him a second bite.

He sat up in his bed and, by and by, he said, "Oh! I'd like another taste of that bird!" So Kate gave him a third bite.

Then he leapt up from his bed, fit and well as ever he was.

In the morning when the king, the queen and the younger brother came, they found Kate and the prince sitting by the fire, cracking nuts and eating them, and rattling on about this and that, like old friends.

The king *was* happy. He said to Kate, "I promised you a bag full of silver and a bag full of gold, and they shall be yours. But that is not enough, for you have done more than watch over my son. You have healed him. So ask for anything you wish."

"Anything?" asked Kate.

"Yes, anything that I have is yours," said the king.

"Then," said Kate, "what I'd like best of all is to marry the prince!"

There, she said it! Kate was not shy.

And the prince? What about him? He was more than willing. He was eager to marry this bright-eyed, lively Kate.

Not long after, the prince's younger brother said that he wanted to marry the other Kate, the bonnie sister who had been bewitched. So, in the end, there was a double wedding. The two Kates married the two brothers.

So there they were again – two Kates in the same family. And it would have been confusing, but the prince who had been sick said that he was going to call his Kate *Kate Crackernuts*, because it was while they sat by the fire cracking hazelnuts that he had first come to know her and love her.

A Scottish tale

THE MAGICAL MERMAID

An English Tale

Reported sightings of a mermaid were quite common among European sailors until a few hundred years ago. She was usually swimming, or sitting on a rock, singing and combing her long hair. As in this English tale, *The Magical Mermaid*, it was considered bad luck to see one. The mermaid could lure a man to his death, or whip up a storm, causing sailors to die at sea.

Lutey is a kind man and his wishes are unusual, because they are so generous. He is saved from the mermaid's enchantment by his barking dog, the sight of his family and finally his knife. The idea that something made of iron might have power over evil was once almost worldwide. It goes back to the time when iron was rare and very valuable. In England iron horseshoes were often hung over doors to protect from witchcraft.

In Greek tales, the siren, a bird-like creature with a woman's head, also enchants men with music, and lures them to their death. The Greek hero Odysseus sails safely past the sirens by having himself bound to his ship's mast and plugging his sailors' ears with beeswax!

KATE CRACKERNUTS

A Scottish Tale

It is unusual in magical tales for step-sisters to be fond of each other and share the same name. Unlike the bossy, selfish and ugly step-sisters in *Cinderella*, plain Kate is thoughtful, loving and kind. She is angry when her step-sister is harmed and, with a determination and resourcefulness that she shows throughout the story, she decides they must run away.

Kate Crackernuts is a story in which fairies play a big role. Like all traditional European fairies, the ones in this Scottish tale have no wings and do not fly. They live under a hill, are ruled by a queen and spend lots of time feasting, dancing and making music. They possess powerful magic and in the story they have put a cruel spell on the prince and, as with Lutey in *The Magical Mermaid*, he cannot escape without outside help. Lutey has iron, the prince has practical Kate, who finds out how to free him from the enchantment.

The end of this story is also unusual. The most *beautiful* girl doesn't win the older prince. Kind, clever Kate is bold enough to ask the prince to marry her. He agrees and then nicknames her *Kate Crackernuts*!

MAGICAL TALES *from* AROUND THE WORLD

Retold by Margaret Mayo ✳ *Illustrated by Peter Bailey*

PEGASUS AND THE PROUD PRINCE
and The Flying Carpet ISBN 1 84362 086 3 £3.99

UNANANA AND THE ENORMOUS ELEPHANT
and The Feathered Snake ISBN 1 84362 087 1 £3.99

THE FIERY PHOENIX
and The Lemon Princess ISBN 1 84362 088 X £3.99

THE GIANT SEA SERPENT
and The Unicorn ISBN 1 84362 089 8 £3.99

THE MAN-EATING MINOTAUR
and The Magic Fruit ISBN 1 84362 090 1 £3.99

THE MAGICAL MERMAID
and Kate Crackernuts ISBN 1 84362 091 X £3.99

THE INCREDIBLE THUNDERBIRD
and Baba Yaga Bony-legs ISBN 1 84362 092 8 £3.99

THE DARING DRAGON
and The Kingdom Under the Sea ISBN 1 84362 093 6 £3.99